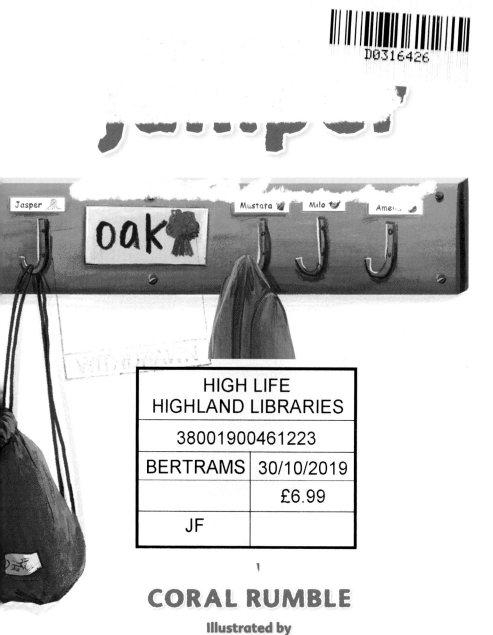

Jasper

Jasper   oak 🎀   Mustafa   Milo   Amelia

CORAL RUMBLE

Illustrated by
Charlotte Cooke

Meet Milo. Milo is in Oak Class.

Just outside Oak Class, on a peg in the cloakroom, a jumper hangs all alone. It's not magic or expensive. It's just a school jumper but, to Milo, it's very important.

Milo likes school
but he feels the opposite of
important. He's not extra clever, or
extra naughty, or extra anything. And
he doesn't get chosen to do things very
often. Unlike his best friend, Eddie, who
always gets chosen to do everything.

It's a Monday morning and the sun is poking its long rays through the kitchen window in Milo's house. Milo doesn't mind sharing the kitchen with the sun. His mum is pouring milk over his cereal. His dog, Gus, sits by his swinging feet. Milo knows that Gus is hoping that some milky cereal will fall, so he can lick it up.

At half past eight, Milo and his mum walk to school. Gus comes too. When Milo has counted fifty flagstones, and Gus has sniffed fifty smells, it means they are nearly at school.

Last Friday, Miss Bennett said a new boy was coming and that he would be joining Milo's class. Miss Bennett said he couldn't speak much English. She asked if someone would sit next to him. Nobody wanted to. Everyone thought being friendly to a boy who doesn't speak much English would be a hard job.

"Eddie, you can do it," said Miss Bennett.
So Eddie HAD
to do it.

Milo walks through the front gate.
The playground is already full of
book bags and lunch boxes.
"Hello, Milo!" shouts Eddie, and
races across the playground to
where Milo is standing.

Eddie puts his scooter in the scooter rack and walks next to Milo. Milo says goodbye to his mum, strokes Gus on the head, and walks in with Eddie.

"I'm nervous about looking after the new boy," says Eddie. "I hope he doesn't turn up."

Milo tries to think of something kind to say to stop his friend from feeling nervous. At last, he says, "The new boy will just be a boy like us, but with different words." This seems to cheer Eddie up.

Milo sits down on his seat at Red Table. He looks across the room at Green Table, where Eddie is sitting. Other children tumble into the classroom, laughing and chatting as they sit down.

There's an empty chair next to Eddie. The new boy is standing at the front. Miss Bennett claps a pattern and everyone copies her. It always makes everyone quiet.

Tuesday
20th

"Good morning, Oak Class," says Miss Bennett. "This is Mustafa." Everyone looks at Mustafa. He seems very shy.

Monday
Tuesday
Wednesday
Thursday
Friday
Saturday

Miss Bennett holds Mustafa's hand, and leads him to Green Table. He sits next to Eddie. Eddie smiles at Mustafa, and Mustafa smiles back. Eddie doesn't seem to know what to do next.

When it's assembly time, Milo stands next to Mustafa in line. He wants to say hello, but he can't remember how to say Mustafa's name.

After assembly, Oak Class do lots of writing. Then they do some shape work. Miss Bennett lets Mustafa write words in his own language.

At break time, Eddie asks Milo to help him play with Mustafa, because he doesn't know how to play with a boy who can't speak much English.

Milo throws his tennis ball to Mustafa, and Mustafa catches it. Mustafa smiles the biggest smile. They make a game where they bounce the ball to each other and have to catch it. Every time one of them drops the ball, they both laugh. They race over to the hopscotch and hop and jump until the whistle blows.

Milo wishes that Miss Bennett had asked him to look after Mustafa. He thinks he would be good at it. Boys from other countries like playing games. Boys from other countries smile and laugh. It really isn't a hard job to be friends with a boy from another country.

The next day, when Milo arrives at school, Miss Bennett asks if Mustafa can sit next to him on Red Table. "I think Mustafa would like that," says Miss Bennett.

Milo feels very important. He doesn't usually get chosen to do things. Mustafa sits next to Milo and smiles a big smile. Milo shows him where he should write his name on his book bag. It really isn't a hard job.

Mustafa is a quick learner. By the start of the next term, he knows lots of English words. He especially likes to write stories. At first, his stories are sad. In one of his stories, some children have to leave their houses because they are in danger. They have to move to another country, just like Mustafa. But after a while, Mustafa's stories have happy endings.

He likes to read them to the class. Some of his stories are very funny! Sometimes Milo and Eddie and the rest of the class laugh and laugh, and Mustafa smiles his big smile.

Some Fridays, Mustafa goes to Milo's house for tea after school. The first time he meets Gus he is a bit scared. Gus dances around him because sometimes dogs get excited. He sniffs Mustafa's legs. Milo knows that Gus isn't scared of Mustafa because boys from other countries smell the same as boys from this country. Mustafa soon gets used to Gus and enjoys throwing the ball for him.

Milo and Mustafa become good friends. When Milo is grumpy, Mustafa pulls a funny face. He can touch his nose with his tongue and go cross-eyed. When Mustafa is sad, Milo just sits next to him and is extra gentle. Sometimes sad people just want you to sit next to them. It's not a hard job.

On Milo's birthday, Mustafa gives him a present. It's a drawing of a dog that looks like Gus. He has put it in a frame. Mustafa is good at drawing. Milo tells him it's the best present ever.

The week before the end of term, Mustafa comes to school a bit late. He looks really, really sad. Milo sits next to him, quietly.
"What's wrong?" Milo asks him at break time.
"I don't want to talk about it," says Mustafa. So they don't.
Instead they race around the playground with Eddie. They dart in and out of everyone else, playing tag, until Mustafa smiles his big smile.

After break, Mustafa's mum knocks on the classroom door. Mustafa stares at his knees. Miss Bennett's eyes are sad and then she looks at the floor. She gives Mustafa's mum a big hug. Milo has never seen Miss Bennett give someone a big hug before. Mustafa's mum leaves the classroom. Her eyes are shiny with tears.

That night, Mustafa and his mum come to Milo's house. Milo plays with Mustafa and his mum talks to Mustafa's mum in the kitchen. Mustafa tells Milo he has to go on an aeroplane with his family, back to his old country.

"Do you have to go for ever and ever?" says Milo.

"Yes," says Mustafa. He looks very sad. Gus sits right by him and licks Mustafa's hand.

At bedtime, Milo asks his mum lots of questions about why Mustafa has to go. When she kisses him goodnight, she says that he has to remember how wonderful it is that he has met Mustafa.

"Mustafa will always be in your memories," she says. "You made that extra effort to be extra friendly and that made Mustafa proud to be your best friend. He chose you because you're a very extra everything kind of boy."
That makes Milo smile a smile as big as Mustafa's smiles.

The next day at school, Milo feels strange. It seems wrong not to have Mustafa sitting next to him. At break, he finds Mustafa's school jumper on the wall bars in the hall. The ends of the sleeves are messy because he used to chew them. Mustafa chewed extra hard when he was thinking and writing stories.

Milo hangs it on the peg next to his, in the cloakroom just outside Oak Class.

It stays there every night all alone, when Milo and his friends have gone home. Mr Sykes, the caretaker, never moves it. He knows it has to hang next to Milo's peg because the friendship between Milo and Mustafa was special. Extra special. The jumper isn't magic or expensive. It's just a school jumper but, to Milo, it's very important. It's Mustafa's jumper.

Who are refugees and migrants?

Sometimes people leave their homes because a war, a natural disaster or terrorism means that it's dangerous to stay. These people are known as refugees. Others leave for a happier, healthier life, or because they don't have enough money and need a job. People who choose to do this are called migrants. Mustafa and his family are migrants.

Refugees and migrants are often so desperate to escape their homes that they risk their lives. Some hide in lorries without food or water, others travel across rough seas in overcrowded boats. Mustafa was lucky and travelled to his new country safely.

By the time they reach their destination, many refugees and migrants have only the clothes they are wearing. It's hard to get help when they don't know who to ask and don't speak the country's language. Milo knew this about Mustafa and knew that he had to be kind and patient with him.

When a refugee or migrant arrives in a new country, they have to ask the government for permission to stay. This is called 'seeking asylum'. When asylum is given, children can go to school where they make new friends and sometimes learn a new language. Mustafa became best friends with Milo.

Not all asylum seekers are allowed to stay. Some are sent back to their home countries. This is what happened to Mustafa and his family.

'Mustafa's Jumper' is based on a poem of the same name by Coral Rumble. This poem won the prestigious Caterpillar Poetry Prize in 2018.

Mustafa's Jumper by Coral Rumble

Mustafa's jumper is alone in the hall,
It hangs from the bars fitted onto the wall.
The sleeve ends are frayed from Mustafa's nibbling,
When he thought very hard, was excitedly scribbling.
His stories were short, but each plot was real,
He told of long journeys, how sad people feel,
But over the weeks, his stories got longer,
The endings were happier, his smile got much stronger.
And Mustafa learnt the language we speak,
And all about book bags and days of the week.
Mustafa was moved to sit next to me,
And sometimes he came to my house for some tea.
Then, one day, Mustafa's mum knocked on the door,
She spoke to Miss Bennett, who stared at the floor.
Mustafa was leaving, the departure was soon,
And an icy anxiety flooded the room.
But it's Mustafa's jumper, it's Mustafa's chair,
It's Mustafa's workbook, and everyone cares
That Mustafa's gone to the airport today,
And right now, this minute, he's flying away.
So, I'll straighten his chair, and picture his face,
Pretend that he's scribbling his stories, with pace,
Then I'll rescue his jumper, and patch up the twine,
And hang it, with love, on the peg next to mine.

Published by
Wacky Bee Books
Shakespeare House, 168 Lavender Hill, London, SW11 5TG, UK

ISBN: 978-1-9999033-5-0

First published in the UK 2019

© 2019 Coral Rumble and Charlotte Cooke

Design by David Rose

Picture credits:
Pixabay.com
Anjo Kan / Orlok / quetions123 / Shutterstock.com

Printed by AkcentMEDIA

www.wackybeebooks.com